This Walker book belongs to :

_____

_____

_____

I'm Numb

For Emz, Else
and Meeli

M.R.

For a couple
of mates,
Oliver and
Cedric

B.G.

Lancashire Library Services

12122741	
PETERS	JF
£5.99	14-Mar-2011

First published 2009 by Walker Books Ltd, 87 Vauxhall Walk, London SE11 5HJ
This edition published 2010 10 9 8 7 6 5 4 3 2 1 Text © 2009 Michael Rosen
Illustrations © 2009 Bob Graham The moral rights of the author and the illustrator
have been asserted. This book has been typeset in Memphis Printed in China
All rights reserved. British Library Cataloguing in Publication Data is available.
ISBN 978-1-4063-2602-4 www.walker.co.uk

er One!

Michael Rosen

illustrated by

Bob Graham

WALKER BOOKS
AND SUBSIDIARIES
LONDON • BOSTON • SYDNEY • AUCKLAND

Let me tell you:
A-One rules.
A-One is number one.
Now, Sally, wind my key."

As Sally wound his key, A-One said,
"Sally, you're no good at winding my key.
Maddy, you do it."

So Maddy wound his key.

But A-One said,
"Maddy, you're hopeless
at it. Sid, you do it."

So Sid wound his key.

But A-One said,
**"Sid, you're useless
at it too."**

Even so, after all that winding,
Sally, Maddy and Sid had
wound up A-One.

A bit later, A-One started pointing at Maddy.
"You look mad in your hat," he said.
And he made up a song, *"Maddy is a mad-hat!"*

Maddy took off her hat.

"Thanks,"
said A-One.
"I'll have that hat."

Then A-One started pointing at Sally.
"Look at you! You wear a rucksack!"
And he sang, *"Sally is a silly-sack!"*

Sally took off her rucksack.

"Good,"
A-One said.
"I'll have this sack."

Then A-One pointed at Sid.
"Siddy is a silly-scarf.
Siddy is a saddy!" he sang.
Sid took his scarf off.

"I'll have your scarf,"
said A-One.

"I'm A-One,"
A-One said.
"I'm big A-One.
Let me tell you:
I'm in charge."

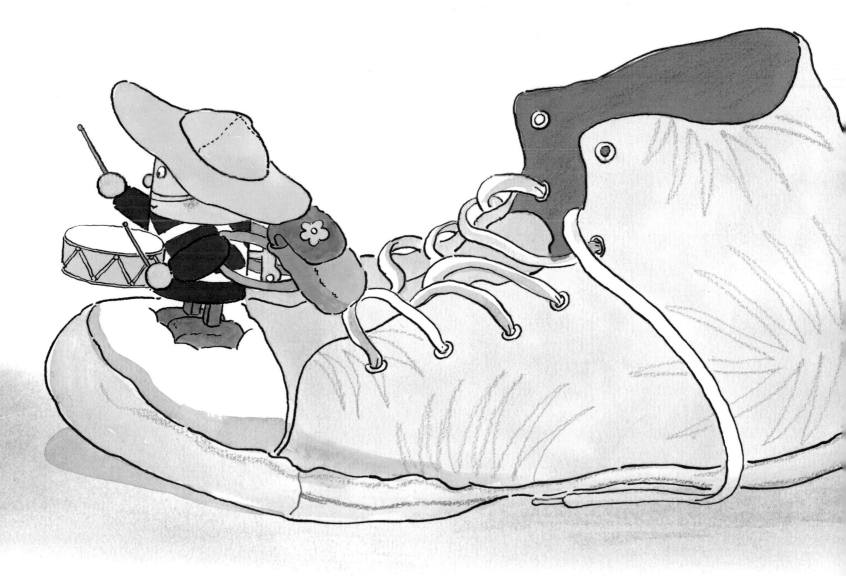

Maddy, Sally and Sid looked
at A-One standing there in the hat,
the rucksack and the scarf...

"Silly-hat and Mad-scarf,"
whispered Sid.

"No, it's 'Silly-scarf' and 'Sad-hat',"
whispered Sally.

"No, it's 'Sad-silly' and 'Bad-mad',"
whispered Maddy.

A-One noticed what was
going on and said,
"You can whisper as
much as you like,
but you're all still no good,
hopeless and useless."

"Hope-use, good-no and less-less," said Sid.
A-One heard him and frowned.

"Less-good, use-hope and less-no,"
giggled Sally.
A-One stamped his foot.

"Hope-no, less-good
and no-less,"
laughed Maddy.

A-One heard what
she said...

He tried not to smile,
but he did.

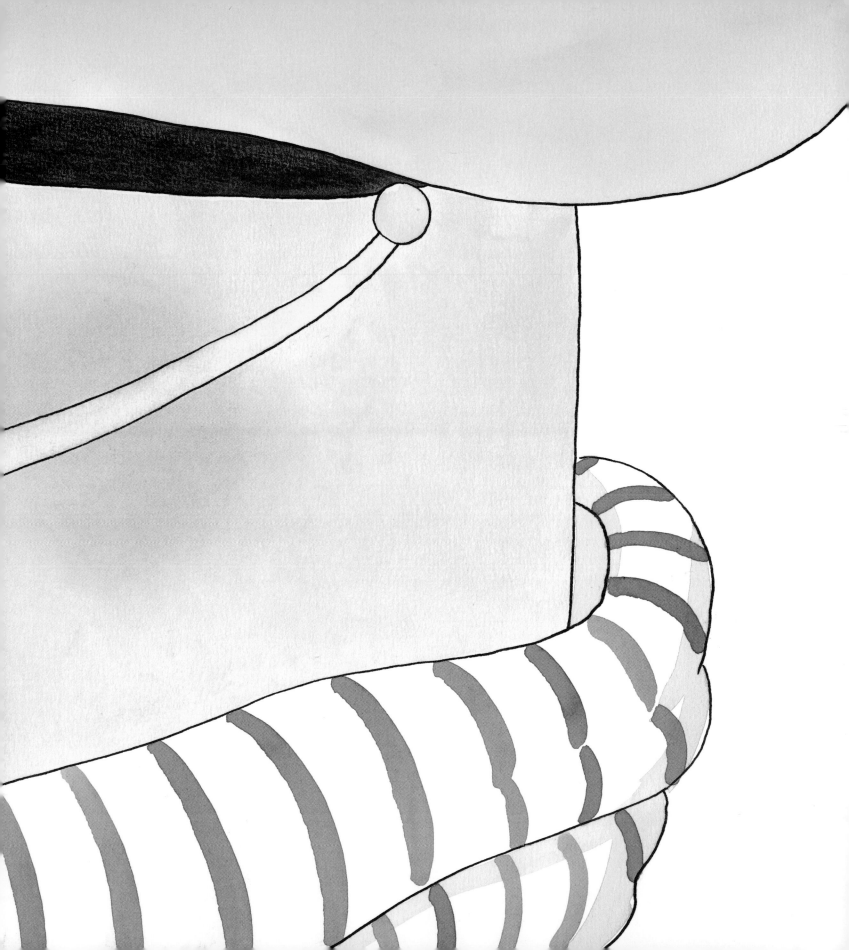

Then Maddy said
to A-One, "Actually, A-One,
we're very good at
winding your key,
aren't we?"

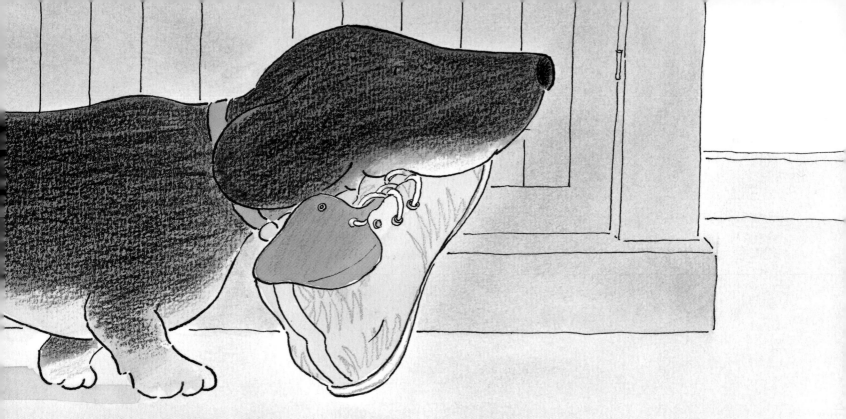

And Sally said, "If we didn't wind your key, you'd be no good."

"You'd be no good, hopeless and useless!" said Sid.

"I'd be a good-less no-no!"
A-One said, and he started
to laugh. He laughed so
much the hat came off.

"Actually," A-One said,
"I could try winding my
key by myself."

Everyone was quiet.
Very quiet.

Then, without saying anything, A-One went over to Maddy and very gently put her hat on her head.

Then he went over to Sally and put her rucksack back on her back, so that it fitted just right.

And then he went over
to Sid and wrapped the
scarf round his neck,
very very carefully.

"I'm A-One,"
A-One said.
"I'm one of
the gang."

ALSO BY **MICHAEL ROSEN** AND **BOB GRAHAM**

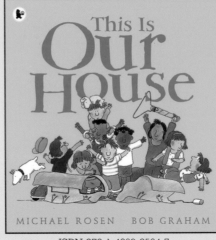

ISBN 978-1-4063-0564-7

OTHER BOOKS BY **MICHAEL ROSEN**

ISBN 978-1-4063-1832-6

ISBN 978-0-7445-2323-2

ISBN 978-0-7445-9800-1

OTHER BOOKS BY **BOB GRAHAM**

ISBN 978-1-4063-2155-5

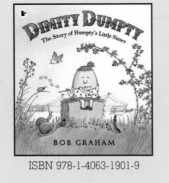

ISBN 978-1-4063-1901-9

ISBN 978-1-4063-2549-2

Available from all good bookstores

www.walker.co.uk
www.walkerbooks.com.au